To Antonia and Rosie
–J.S.

To Mum, Dad, and James. You know you're in it!
–M.W.

tiger tales
an imprint of ME Media, LLC
202 Old Ridgefield Road
Wilton, CT 06897
First published in the United States 2007
Originally published in Great Britain 2007
by Hodder Children's Books
a division of Hachette Children's Books, London

CIP data is available
ISBN-13: 978-1-58925-069-7
ISBN-10: 1-58925-069-9
First U.S. edition
Printed in China

1 3 5 7 9 10 8 6 4 2

That Pesky Dragon
by Julie Sykes
Illustrated by
Melanie Williamson
tiger tales

IZZIE'S DAD HAD A FARM.

And on that farm there was a herd of cows...

some chickens . . .
three cats . . .
two dogs . . .
and a dragon!

It didn't take everyone long to realize that there was a dragon on the farm—its fierce roar gave it away!

When Izzie stood on tiptoes and peered out of her window, she could just see the tip of the dragon's tail by the well on top of the hill.

Rrrrooooaaaarrrr!

"Can we go and look at it?" asked Izzie.

"Certainly not," said Dad. "Dragons are far too dangerous. If we leave it alone, it'll be gone by tomorrow."

But the next morning, it was the roar of the dragon and not the rooster that woke Izzie from her cozy dream.

"It's still here," thought Izzie, secretly pleased.

But she was in for a shock when she went out into the cold to gather the eggs for breakfast.

"These eggs feel rock hard!" said Izzie, as she shivered her way around the henhouse.

"It's that pesky dragon," said Grandpa, angrily. "His fiery breath has hard-boiled the eggs!"

Izzie was desperate to see the dragon, but Mom wouldn't hear of it.

"That dragon's a mean one. You can tell from its roar," she said.

“I think it sounds sad,” said Izzie. “Can’t I take a tiny peek?”

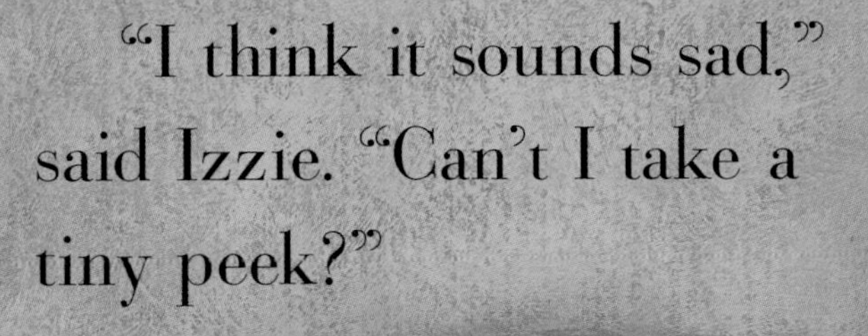

Rrrroooaaaarrrr!

“Definitely not,” said Mom. “Go inside and with luck it’ll fly away soon.”

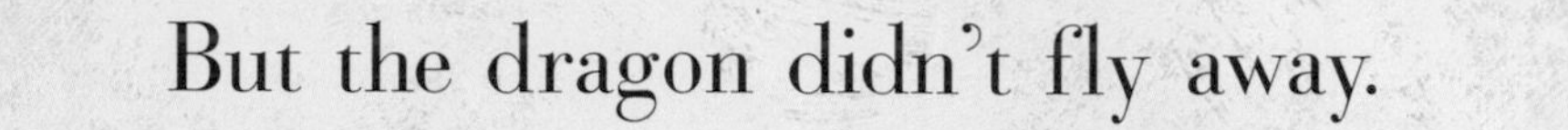

That afternoon, when Izzie went outside to help Mom milk the cows, they were in for another shock.

"Yogurt!" cried Izzie.

"Oh, dear," said Mom. "It's that pesky dragon's fault. Its roaring has scared the cows and turned their milk to yogurt!"

Rrrroooaaaarrrr!

The next morning, it was the light of the dragon's fiery breath and not the light of the rising sun that woke Izzie. A lovely smell was drifting up the stairs.

"Mmm, toast," cried Izzie, sliding down the banister.

"It's not toast. It's my prize wheat!" Dad said bitterly. "That pesky dragon burned a whole field in the night. This can't go on. I'm calling REMOVE-A-DRAGON!"

“Not REMOVE-A-DRAGON!” shrieked Izzie. “Why don’t you just ask the dragon to leave?”

“It’s far too dangerous,” said Dad, picking up the phone. “It’s fierce, that dragon. Just listen to its roar.”

“It sounds hurt, not fierce, if you ask me,” said Izzie.

“Run along now while I make this call,” said Dad.

Rrrroooaaaarrrr!

So Izzie ran. She ran out of the farmhouse, past the chicken coop, through the cow pasture, and all the way up the hill toward the dragon....

Suddenly, Izzie was scared.

What if the dragon was dangerous?

What if it was hungry?

What if it ate little girls for breakfast?

She panicked.

But it was too late.
The dragon had
already seen her.

Gulp!

Izzie took a brave step forward. She could see the scales on its tail and feel the heat of its breath.

But the big, roaring, scary dragon was just a tiny dragon trapped in the well and crying for help.

"I've been shouting for help for days!"
the dragon cried.

Izzie ran back down the hill and got Mom, Dad, Grandpa, and the REMOVE-A-DRAGON lady to help.

"They look scary," whispered the dragon, as they marched toward him.

"Don't worry," said Izzie. "Sit still and don't breathe or you might singe us when we pull you out!"

The dragon held his breath while Izzie, the REMOVE-A-DRAGON lady, Mom, Dad, and Grandpa pulled, and pulled, and pulled until…

Pop!
The dragon was free!

Now Izzie's dad has a farm with a herd of cows...

a flock of sheep...

some chickens...

three cats...

a goat...

two dogs...

and a dragon!

And now Izzie loves cold mornings. With a dragon around, there's always hot milk, hard-boiled eggs, and toast for breakfast!

MILK